# THE WITCHSLAYER

## THE OKRITH NOVELLAS
### BOOK THREE

A.K. MULFORD

Paperback 978-0-473-61652-6

Ebook 978-0-473-61653-3

Publisher AK Mulford

2021

New Zealand

Cover by MiblArt

Map by Holly Dunn Designs

Interior Formatting by K. Elle Morrison

# CONTENT WARNING

This book contains themes of violence, torture, loss, and allusion to sexual assault.

**Spoiler Warning**

This novella contains spoilers from The Five Crowns of Okrith Book 2, The Witches' Blade.

CHAPTER ONE

T he door slammed, and Renwick jolted awake. Wiping the sticky, drool-covered cards off his cheek, he squinted against the rays of morning light. Flurries of snow danced across the frosted windowpane, winter still clinging to spring.

"Gods," he groaned, rubbing a hand down his face. He must have dozed off while playing cards with Thador . . . again.

A high voice came from the doorway. "The maid is about to inform you that the stable boy has saddled your horse."

Silhouetted in the bright light was Aneryn. The young girl stood with her arms folded, her dark brown skin haloed against the morning sunlight. Her short hair was braided up to a line of puffs like the crest of a soldier's helmet—her own sort of armor against the world.

"How long do I have?" Renwick asked, frowning down at his crumpled tunic.

Aneryn's eyes flared sapphire blue before returning to their warm brown. "I'm not a clock, but soon."

She scowled as Thador popped up from the far side of the table.

Shirtless, his torso of golden-brown skin was covered in

1

old battle scars, minor compared to the puckering wound that ran down his face. His head nearly skimmed the rafters, and he placed his hands flat on the ceiling as he stretched.

"Ah, good, you're here," Renwick mumbled as Thador pulled his tunic over his head and leaned down, helping up someone from the ground.

Obscured behind the card table, Renwick hadn't seen the woman lying beside Thador. As she stood, he noted it was one of the courtesans from the tavern next door. They spent most evenings hanging around the back doors of the tavern, getting some fresh air before their long nights in the throng of drunken patrons.

"Well, I guess I'll be going then," she said, adjusting her bosom and tightening her corset. She was short and plump, half the size of Thador, and yet with a confidence that took up the whole room.

"See you around, Tilly," Thador said, pulling her by the hip back to him and planting a kiss on her brunette hair. He passed another coin pouch from the side table to her.

Narrowing her eyes at the money, she patted her skirts, which jangled with coins. "You've already paid me three times as much as my going rate."

Thador guffawed as she extended the coins back to him. "I know you don't need it, but it saves me from spending all my earnings on too much ale." He didn't reach to take the coin purse back, so she shrugged and put it in her pockets.

"Well, in that case." She combed a finger through her matted hair as she gave Thador a wink. "I'm not looking for some chivalrous knight to rescue me. Having a rollick with an ogre like you is more fun than working in the kitchens. My auntie is the head seamstress for the Brufdoran Clothiers . . . but why would I want to spend my days being stuck by needles, when I could be s—"

Renwick's pointed cough silenced her before she could continue. He tipped his head to Aneryn, who was lingering by the door. The young witch looked exasperated already.

Though none of this discussion was anything new to her. She knew much darker parts of the world than this lewd conversation, despite his efforts to protect her.

With a booming laugh, Thador placed another wanton kiss on her cheek as Tilly surveyed the room for something.

Pinching the bridge of her nose, Aneryn pointed to the corner where a wool garment was draped across an armchair.

Besotted, Thador watched as Tilly grabbed her shawl and shoes. It was true, courtesans were often looked down upon, and yet the shrewd ones were some of the wealthiest people in any town. Their businesses never went out of fashion, and they always had patrons willing to pay their weight in gold for their attentions.

Renwick couldn't understand it though—why all the fae males he knew were so driven by their ardor. They all seemed so frenzied and urgent . . . and it made him wonder if a part of him didn't exist. Why wasn't he constantly enflamed by desire like Thador, his father, and the rest of them? He'd had a few pleasurable dalliances with ladies, and yet, no urgency to repeat it. Everyone else seemed crazed on this drug called lust.

"It's been fun." Tilly waved over her shoulder as she padded barefoot toward the door. "Come find me if you need another distraction."

Aneryn stepped further into the room, giving Tilly a wide berth to pass. Renwick glanced at the leather collar around the blue witch's neck, a stone hanging from it, carved with the Northern Court crest. Many were enslaved to rich fae, and the most talented went to the harem of his father, the Northern King. Unlike what Tilly had, there was no free will there. It wasn't much of a blessing, but at least there were so many of them that they could share the burden. He did not know how many decades it would be until he became King, but the moment he did, the harem would be disbanded.

He prayed the collars still pained him too—that it still

made him ache to see them encircling witches' necks. He clenched his fists at his side, time and fear wearing down his resolve. Perhaps one day, it would all just feel normal to him. Perhaps he would stop questioning the status quo at all.

A memory flashed before his eyes . . . no, not a memory. It was a memory yet to occur. Biting down on the inside of his cheek until he tasted blood, the flash of roses in the rain faded from his mind's eye.

"You okay?" Thador asked as Renwick kept his eyes screwed shut.

"Breathe," Aneryn commanded as her footsteps grew closer and she sat in the chair beside him.

Taking a deep, shuddering breath, Renwick opened his eyes again even as his heartbeat thumped in his ears. It was getting out of hand. This panic would defeat him.

"I should come with you today," Thador said, rubbing his jaw with worry.

"No," Renwick snapped. "It's bad enough I brought you with me to Murreneir, but you can't go near the blue witch fortress. One look at your snarky face and Balorn will have a knife in your throat." He slid his eyes to Aneryn, who was leaning against the doorframe. "Besides, I need you to keep an eye on her."

Aneryn rolled her eyes. "I don't need a babysitter." The sound of hasty footsteps sounded from the stairwell as Aneryn gestured to the door. "That'll be the maid."

Renwick hunted for his boots, finding them discarded under the card table. He yanked them on as a brief knock sounded at the door.

Aneryn answered, opening the door a sliver.

"His Highness's horse is ready and waiting outside," a mousy voice sounded from the gap.

"He will be down shortly," Aneryn replied curtly in lilting Ific. She had an elegant fae accent, so unlike the other witches. She had spent most of her life with Renwick and Thador, hiding in the fringes of royal fae life. Renwick knew

4

how the other witches looked at her, like she was a traitor. But at least she was safe.

He tied the laces with practiced hands as Aneryn paced over to him.

"Don't forget this," she said, extending out his flask.

Glancing at the silver container, his chest tightened, but he took it. He would inevitably need its contents if he was venturing into the blue witch fortress.

"I hate this," Thador growled. "All of this. We need to find you some backcountry gambling hall and stay there until your father dies of old age."

Renwick huffed, standing to tie his dagger to his belt. "I'd like nothing more."

"I'll think of something." Thador helped him into his riding coat before spinning Renwick around and holding him by the shoulders. He gave Renwick a hard look and said, "We *will* survive this."

Renwick wanted to break at those words, wanted to crumple to the floor as he had done that day years ago in Drunehan when his guard had delivered the news—his mother and brother had died. But he remained as still as a stone, pushing down hard on those emotions rising within him. Every day he slipped further below the surface of those waves. It wouldn't be long before he was drowning. Maybe he already was.

He clapped his guard on the shoulder, his only acknowledgment of his words. Giving Aneryn a brief nod, he left. As he paced down the hallway of the inn, he braced himself for another day in the underworld.

# CHAPTER TWO

The pathways were treacherous, slick with patches of ice. As the warming sun melted the persisting snow-drifts, the morning chill froze them again, creating jagged banks. Winter warred with spring. Soon green stalks would be jutting up through the snow, a promise of warmer weather.

Framed through an open archway, pillars of smoke rose from between the undulating hills in the far distance. Renwick peered back over the barren landscape to the obscured town he'd departed from. The people of Murreneir had just moved back into their homes, having wintered on the ice lakes. Just like the new shoots of springtime flowers, the pilgrimage back to Murreneir marked the change of seasons like clockwork. There was something comforting about that steady rhythm, that no matter what, the flowers would bloom and the people would return to Murreneir.

Taking another careful step along the slippery path, Renwick stared beyond the valley of Murreneir to a flattened hillside above it. His gut clenched. His mother had decided to build a spring palace on that naked mountain, cleared of trees. He wondered how many decades it would take before the forest reclaimed the building site now that she was dead.

He turned away, hardening his heart as he navigated the cliff edge past the dormitories to the main building.

Passing the stoic faces of half-frozen guards, Renwick entered his uncle's office on the top floor. Warmth burned his frosted cheeks and nose, a fire roaring with life in the corner of the decorous room. Gilded regalia and tapestries hung from the stone walls, framing the large mahogany desk.

Wiping his boots on the rough mat under the doorframe, Renwick stepped onto the plush cobalt carpet.

Balorn looked up from his stack of papers and stood with a smile. He wore his usual uniform: a double-breasted jacket made of rough gray fabric with golden buttons and matching epaulets denoting his rank. He was the commander of the soldiers who ran the blue witch fortress and a Prince of the Northern Court. Giving Balorn a job had been the smartest thing his father, Hennen, had ever done. At first, Balorn was tasked with breaking the blue witches, but now that Yexshire had fallen, he had an even more important job—break the blood magic bound to the Immortal Blade.

Scattered across the giant desktop were history books and spell books and, beside them, stacks of scribbled notes. Even after several years, Balorn was still doggedly determined to break the magic controlling the Immortal Blade. His experiments had grown even more unruly as he pushed the blue witches ever harder to reveal their visions in a desperate bid for more information.

"I was wondering when you'd arrive," Balorn admonished, shuffling through his papers and selecting one.

Balorn had auburn hair streaked with the same red as his father's when the light hit it just right, but he was more handsome than the Northern King. Despite being only a few years younger than his brother, he looked youthful and charming, having cared for himself much better.

Fae lifespan was different than that of witches and humans. The middle of their lives could stretch on and on for decades, unlike the others. But Renwick's father loved drinking and revelry and aged at a similar rate to the humans around him. Renwick suspected Balorn plied his brother with wine and greasy meats so that he would fade long before him. It created an unending tension between the two of them. Renwick wondered if his uncle was circling like a vulture over the throne and if he viewed his nephew as an obstacle toward his ultimate goal. Even though Renwick was the Crown Prince, he feared what his uncle might do to him. But he could never confirm it. All he knew was that when Hennen died, he wanted to be as far away from Balorn as possible.

"Forgive me, Uncle," Renwick said. "The roads are icy with the cold front, and the ride from Murreneir took longer than I expected today."

"You should reside here in the fortress with me, Witchslayer," Balorn offered for the hundredth time. "Not in that shithole town."

"Thank you for the offer, Uncle," Renwick said obediently, but he always turned his uncle down.

"Suit yourself." Balorn shrugged, scanning Renwick with piercing forest green eyes. "Staying up too late drinking?"

"No, Uncle," Renwick replied, smoothing his hand down his wrinkled, stained tunic.

"You are only young once, Witchslayer. Have your fun." Balorn snickered. "But when you come here, be ready to work and look the part."

Renwick took the piece of paper from his outstretched hand. "Yes, Uncle."

"This is your legacy," he said, tapping his knuckles into the tapestry behind him painted with the Northern crest. He slammed his fist into the tapestry again, the coiled snake rippling on the fabric. "Are you listening?"

This was Balorn—charming one minute, erratic and violent the next. Everyone stayed alert around him because he had a vicious bloodlust and killed with a smile.

"You are a Vostemur, made of iron and venom, don't you

9

forget that," Balorn snarled as Renwick bobbed his chin. "The Berecrafts were weak," he added, making Renwick swallow a lump in his throat. "Prove to your father that weakness doesn't flow through your veins like it did in your brother."

Renwick held completely still, hoping it made him seem uncaring. Berecraft was his mother's maiden name. It had been three years since his mother and brother had died, and he still didn't know where they were buried, if they were buried at all.

The Northern Queen had tried to flee Drunehan along with her younger son, Eadwin, and had been discovered. The idea was laughable. Where could she possibly go that the Vostemur army couldn't find her? It was only weeks after her death that his father laid waste to the High Mountain Court and the witch hunts began. Renwick always wondered how much of it was triggered by his mother's abandonment. Of course, his father wasn't the only one she abandoned—she left Renwick behind as well. The Northern Court never knew what truly happened to them. The lie that they died from a sudden illness rolled easily enough off Hennen's tongue, but Renwick's father had told him the truth. Traitors and deserters weren't remembered. No day of mourning was held. No stones were placed in their honor. They were gone and the world moved on.

Balorn reached across the desk and tapped the paper in Renwick's hand. "This one is new. Welcome her."

The paper was blank apart from the number 14, a date, and a name: Gemma Benton. She would be on the third level down. They'd frighten her with a week of training, send her to the dormitories to heal her wounds, then drag her back again.

Renwick swallowed the lump in his throat. If he was ever going to survive his father's court, he needed to get used to this. This was who his family was; he was the heir to these nightmares.

"I see knives have not been used yet." Renwick looked up

to his uncle with a twisted smile, one he knew would make his uncle proud. "Let's see if we can get this Gemma Benton to talk."

"It's good to see you are not soft-hearted like your brother." Moving around the desk, Balorn playfully smacked him on the back. "You are a monster, my Witchslayer."

Shrieks and sobs echoed down the corridor as he navigated towards his assigned room. Loosening his collar, he took a breath of the stale air. Each step in the belly of the fortress was more suffocating than the last. One door was left ajar . . . not #14. Pausing, he wondered which guard had left it open.

Reaching for the handle, he peered at the witch strung up by manacles. Her silver hair spilled over her shoulders as she stared under heavy brows. One eye was purpled and swollen, her skin blotched in bruises. But her glare wasn't one of misery and defeat; rather, it was filled with violent mischief.

"Little Witchslayer," she beckoned in a singsong voice. "I have stories to tell you. Come play with me."

Renwick took a step into the room. Grabbing the handle, he warned, "You better knock that off if you don't want Forgotten One carved into your forehead."

He hid his shudder, thinking of the creatures kept locked in the bowels of the mountain. He hated going down there. Some were completely lifeless, limp and unspeaking, barely rousing enough to eat. Others were erratic and violent, having to be kept permanently shackled. And this witch in front of him was beginning to get the look in her eyes . . . the one that showed she had slipped beyond the pale. Yet another one lost to the depths of this keep. He was certain Balorn did it on purpose—pushed them too hard so that he could keep some for himself.

His uncle called it *the menagerie*. Every new witch sent to train would be given a tour of the eerie pit: a warning to behave. Everyone feared becoming another one of Balorn's pets, even the guards. Whenever Renwick stepped foot in the main building, he wondered if he'd get locked away like the others. If his uncle ever discovered his secrets, he surely would be.

"Your warnings are hollow," the witch cackled. "I will not survive this place, Witchslayer. Come, let me whisper in your ear."

"Rest," Renwick commanded, yanking the door shut. "You will need it."

The witch laughed as he double-checked the lock.

A guard carrying a slop bucket clung to the far wall as he passed.

"You!" Renwick seethed, pointing at him.

The guard halted with a jolt, the putrid liquid sloshing over the lip of the bucket onto his boots. He didn't acknowledge it, just stared wide-eyed at Renwick. This is how they all saw him: The Witchslayer, protégée to his uncle and equally as lethal.

"Why was this door left unlocked?" Renwick snarled, pointing to the door. The mask he wore slipped so easily over his face, the countenance starting to become more and more of whom he truly was.

"I-I don't know, Your Highness," the guard stammered as his cheeks flushed crimson red. He couldn't have been more than sixteen. It was smart of Balorn to start them so young, establishing loyalties to him above anyone else, even their families.

"Isn't it your job to know?" Renwick asked, narrowing his eyes.

The guard blanched. "I can go ask Fowler?"

Fowler, the head guard and son of the Lord of Vurstyn, had been promoted through name. Balorn and the Lord were old friends, and Balorn had swiftly offered a position for the younger Fowler in his retinue.

"See that you do," Renwick hissed, glaring at the guard's stained boots.

Fowler worked far across the fortress, which would mean this guard would be gone a while. The guard bobbed his head and scurried down the hallway.

The acrid stench of blood and bile lingered in the stale air as he reached the handle of his assigned room. Dropping his shoulders and lifting his chin, he steadied himself for what was to come. It was a necessary act, he promised, as he shoved away all the good parts left of himself.

# CHAPTER THREE

The door creaked open, and a witch lifted her head. She lay trembling in the chilled air, tied to a table. A waif, she still had the round face of a child. Witches were being sent younger and younger for their training. Renwick didn't know which was a worse fate—to be trapped in the fortress for the next several years or to graduate only to be sent to one of the many Northern Lords. Bile rose in his throat.

Weeping wounds covered her exposed arms and legs. She strained against the belts holding her down, but they didn't budge. Her blonde hair was cropped close to the scalp, patches already missing from whoever previously worked on her.

"Please," she whispered, tears falling straight down from her eyes to her ears.

"You must be new here," Renwick said, steeling himself for what was to come. Unbuttoning his cloak, he draped it over her shaking body. "When did you arrive?"

"Two weeks ago, Your Highness." Her bottom lip wobbled as her wide eyes tracked him.

Renwick skimmed his fingers across the side table of rusty instruments, clenching his jaw so tightly he thought his teeth might break. More witches died from infections and fevers than any other torment. Only the strongest survived. Those highly-trained witches were sent to the nobles in every corner of the Northern Court or to join his father's harem in Drunehan.

Renwick sat in the chair in the corner, dropping his head in his hands, another headache building inside his skull. The pressure was so great he thought his eyes might bug out.

"Please," the witch sobbed again.

"Quiet," Renwick growled, rubbing his hands in his eye sockets. "I will ask the questions and you will answer, nothing more. Understood?" The witch nodded. "Good, now, Gemma, tell me. How old were you when you had your first vision?"

"Six, maybe seven?" The witch craned her neck back to look at him. Her eyes fizzled between glowing sapphire and their regular sky blue. "But they have been coming more regularly in the past few years."

"How old are you?"

"Fourteen," she whispered. "How old are you?"

Renwick slammed his hand on the table beside him, and the instruments clanged together, making the girl jump.

"Sorry," she stammered, pressing her lips tightly together.

"Do you summon your visions, or do they just come to you?"

"Both," she said, looking straight up to the ceiling. "I have them in dreams sometimes, and sometimes they come to me when a great danger is about to occur. I had a vision right before the soldiers came for me. I tried to run, but . . ."

Renwick rested his chin in his hands. "Interesting."

He wondered how many witches saw their capture before the soldiers came. How many escaped into the wild woods west of Drunehan? He knew Raevenport was harboring witches, some even skirting over the borders to beg protection from the other courts. His father was losing patience with the other royal families. Battles along the borders in Falhampton and Valtene were breaking out. They were pushing their borders south, controlling the witches' passages to freedom. Many of the courts were wise enough to lie and say they saw no such witches, but the High Mountain Court had refused to return the blue witches who fled into their kingdom . . . and look at them now. The Siege of Yexshire tempered the resistance of the other courts.

His father was arrogant, but the High Mountain King and Queen were absolute fools. They had no defenses that night in Yexshire, their one talisman of power kept hidden away on a sacred altar. If only the Queen thought to carry the Immortal Blade, the battle would have ended very differently. Let it be a lesson to the other courts—trust no one, even allies. It taught them another important thing about the Immortal Blade's magic as well: no blade could pierce the wielder's skin, but they could still be killed. Now the High Mountain Court was nothing but ash. He wondered if the ones who had fled out the windows made it to the woods.

"Are you asleep?" Gemma whispered.

Renwick sneered. "If I was, why would you wake me? Wouldn't you rather your tormentors sleep?"

"I'm sorry," she murmured. The girl was in for a tough journey, one he wasn't sure she would survive. She had too much spirit for a place like this. She needed to learn to hide it away.

Renwick hoped he would be sent to Falhampton next, not back to the capital. He'd rather oversee the uneasy peace. The stalemate at the border had been going on for years. Prince Hale of the Eastern Court would receive him. The Bastard Prince and Renwick had never been friends, but there was a begrudging respect there. They were both the weapons of their fathers, neither able to carve their own path in the world. Raffiel had understood him too, wherever he was in the world now. Renwick feared every day that someone had noticed what he had done during the Siege of Yexshire. He tried to make it look like confusion, getting in between his soldiers and the High Mountain Prince, buying time for him to escape. Chaos had erupted all around them—flames and screams—but if anyone saw . . .

The sound of the witch's whimper pulled him back into his body.

"What's your most recent vision?" Renwick asked.

"A blizzard, Your Highness."

"Stop with the titles," Renwick gritted out. "Save your breath."

Gemma nodded, watching him with wide eyes. Her fear thickened the air, pulsing out of her throughout the room, fingertips and eyes glowing with magical blue flames.

"Can you control the flames?" Renwick gestured to her hands. "Can you put them out even when you're afraid?"

She shook her head. "I hadn't thought to try."

"Try now," he commanded.

Gemma swallowed the lump in her throat. Screwing her eyes shut, the flames flickered out. She held it for a moment before releasing her magic, the flames shooting back to her hands. "It's hard to control." She panted as the tension left her body.

"What does it feel like? To control it?"

"It comes from the center of my chest," she breathed. "Like I'm pushing my lungs out of my body. It's awful."

Rubbing his hand down his face, he asked, "More awful than what they do to you here?"

"No."

Deep voices echoed from down the hall, snapping both of their attention to the closed door.

"You will need to keep practicing it," Renwick said quickly, rising to stand. He pulled a flask from his pocket, holding it to her lips. "Drink this." Gemma gagged, turning her face from the foul scent. Panic rose in his voice as he heard the sounds of boots trudging down the hall. "Do it. Now."

He cupped his hand behind her neck to help lift her head. Grimacing, she swallowed two big gulps before Renwick pulled the flask from her lips.

"Good," he said, hastily putting the flask back in his pocket and pulling out his dagger. Gemma's chest heaved, tears welling in her eyes again as he loomed over her. "Now, scream for me."

Her mouth fell open. "What?"

"Scream," he commanded, lifting his blade and stabbing it down into the table beside her head.

She shrieked, a frightened wail that echoed off the stones and rang in his ears. The sound abruptly ceased as her eyes rolled back and her body went limp, the sleeping tonic taking hold.

Renwick's stomach roiled as he yanked his cloak off her and threw it onto the chair. He quickly sliced his dagger down her cheek, blood beading from the shallow wound. His will to survive at all had begun to wane with each passing day, and now with each movement, his soul fractured into smaller pieces. He dragged his blade down her jaw as the door behind him creaked open.

"Is she out?" Balorn's voice called behind him with a chuckle. "And you're still going? You vicious little thing."

Balorn walked over to him, surveying the fresh slices across the witch's face.

Renwick grabbed her cheeks in his large hand and shook her head, but she didn't rouse. He slapped his hand hard across her face, leaving a red outline of his bloodied palm. He wiped his sanguine fingers down his trousers and shrugged.

"So eager." Balorn's laugh was low and rough. "You've got to ease them into it. Jump scares are fun, but no work will get done with them passing out so quickly." He clapped him on the shoulder. "You'll get the hang of it. Come, let's have lunch."

Renwick wiped his dagger on his tunic and sheathed it back to his hip. "No point without the screams, anyway."

"That's my boy." Balorn grinned at him with more pride than his father had ever shown him.

# CHAPTER FOUR

The dining room peered out over the western ledge of the fortress to the sweeping mountain vistas. Echoes bounced around the cold stone room as they sat in their bloodied clothes eating lunch. Two plates had appeared from the kitchens the instant they sat, the green witches always ready to serve them. The two witches' eyes were impossibly wide as they set the plates down. Even though they weren't blue witches, they still weren't safe from Balorn's temper. How many green witches had lost their lives because they set a plate down too noisily? The witches hastily retreated, safe for another day, leaving them to their meal.

As Renwick reached for his goblet, Balorn placed his hand over the rim.

"I think you've had enough drink today." Balorn's eyebrow quirked up. "Don't think I don't notice that flask in your pocket." His gaze dropped to the table as if he could stare straight through it to Renwick's concealed flask.

Renwick shrugged, pushing the goblet away, even as his heart hammered. Better his uncle think he was a drunk than a traitor.

"You're being sent south," Balorn said as he speared at the fish on his plate. Freshly caught from the ice lakes, he swirled it in the maple glaze. "You'll go with that soldier friend of yours—what's his name?"

"Thador Eloris," Renwick replied through a mouthful of leek and onion tart. He tried to hide his excitement, certain that Thador had some part in these new arrangements.

Balorn hummed in acknowledgment. "Your father wants you to go south, searching around Silver Sands Harbor."

"The south doesn't take kindly to witch hunters."

Balorn waved his hand in dismissal. "They will learn their lesson; Norwood will see to that."

Interest perked, Renwick leaned in. "What does the Eastern King have planned for the Southern Court?"

"All in good time." Balorn chuckled. "Norwood and his witches have been tying strings in the south for years. Pull the right thread, and the whole court will crumble."

"I thought the Eastern King was our enemy," Renwick said, pushing the tart around his plate.

"Norwood wants to make a show with Falhampton, show he's trying." Balorn lifted his goblet to his lips. "But he would not mind one bit if we slaughtered his armies stationed there . . . In fact, he'd probably welcome it."

"Why?"

Balorn smiled wickedly above the rim of his cup. "You are not a fool, Witchslayer. Why do you think? Who commands his armies there?"

"Hale." Renwick blanched. There had been a time they had all been friends, when they were children: Hale, Raffiel, and himself—the crown princes of three kingdoms, pretending to be kings, forming alliances of fealty with each other even then. The world had torn them apart.

"Why would Gedwin want to keep that bastard now that his Fated is gone? He gains nothing by keeping him alive." Balorn laughed as he patted the corners of his mouth with a napkin. "We're doing him a favor by killing the lad. Norwood will have the bleeding hearts of his people and his Queen's heir on the throne."

"And what of our armies stationed there? So far, it seems we are the ones with more casualties . . ."

"We have more to replace them." Balorn shrugged, giving Renwick a stern look. "You are thinking like a soldier, not like a King. It is immaterial how many of them die, so long as we get what we want. We will chip away bit by bit into each court until all of Okrith bows to the Vostemur crown."

Swallowing, Renwick bobbed his head. He had heard this story so many times over the years, hardened more and more to the truth that lay before him. His father and uncle would conquer the realm . . . and he would inherit it. Horror seeped into his bones. He would inherit this nightmare.

"So, to Silver Sands then?" Renwick finally spoke, his voice scratchy, haunted by the future rapidly unfurling before him.

"Yes, there's a silver mine out there. You'll be staying with Hemarr while you go on your hunts."

Renwick recognized the name. Bern Hemarr was a courtier around the same age as him, always flitting from court to court. Bern loved to gamble as much as Renwick, and he'd find Bern popping up at all of the same card games. The silver-haired sycophant was hard to pin down though, never staying in one court for long. Renwick wouldn't be surprised if he was still hidden in the back of the same gambling hall he left him in.

"I will prepare to depart within the week." Renwick blotted the corners of his mouth with his napkin, trying to sound casual.

Balorn propped his elbows on the table, considering Renwick. "Might I suggest you leave your blue witch behind?"

Tightening his expression, he maintained a calculated neutral one, having practiced hiding his tells over the years. Balorn was a keen observer and would note the slightest flicker of muscle.

"Aneryn will come with us to Silver Sands," Renwick

countered. He already didn't like bringing her to Murreneir. It was too close to the blue witch fortress. He left her cloistered in her room during the day with a mountain of books for company. Thador would keep an eye on her.

"You indulge that girl too much," Balorn snapped. "She would benefit from some training."

Renwick held his uncle's gaze, forcing a grin onto his face even as his stomach clenched. "Let me have my pet."

Balorn snickered. "Training her in other ways, then?" The far door opened and one of the trembling green witches from earlier entered, bearing a pitcher of wine to refill Balorn's cup, as he continued. "Fine, bring your plaything with you to Silver Sands. You'll have easy access to the Western and Southern borders from there. A good jumping-off point for those who fled into the foothills of the High Mountains."

The witch's hands shook so badly as she poured, a droplet of wine missed the goblet and splashed onto the table. Time seemed to freeze as all eyes fell on the red liquid pooling on the wood. In a flash, Balorn's hand lashed out, smacking the witch across the face. The clay pitcher fell from her hands, shattering on the hard floor. A dagger was in Balorn's hands as the witch screamed, lifting her hands to shield her face.

"Uncle," Renwick cut in as Balorn threw back his chair and seized the witch by the collar with his free hand.

Balorn paused, looking over his shoulder at his nephew, his knife still raised.

"We are down to two green witches," Renwick said, tossing his napkin on the table, appetite gone. "Will you at least send for more before killing this one? I care not one *druni* for a witch's life, but I'd rather not eat slop. Why punish us for the foolishness of the girl?"

Balorn guffawed, shrugging his shoulders and sheathing his blade. "I suppose there is wisdom in you yet, Witchslayer." He kicked the witch, and she yelped, hustling back into the kitchens.

The far door burst open, and a soldier entered carrying a heavy black sack in his hands. Renwick's heart leapt into his throat as the soldier unceremoniously dropped the bag on the table with a wet smack.

"More witch heads for you, Your Highness," the soldier said with a swift bow and turned to leave.

The stench of rot overwhelmed the savory aromas of their lunch as Balorn smiled at the sack. He inhaled deeply as if savoring the decaying stench. More red witch heads for him to experiment with. He had been using them with a variety of blue witch spells, so far to not much success. They sacked the Temple of Yexshire for the red witches' spell books, but nothing was working to unbind the magic of the Immortal Blade.

"When you go to Silver Sands . . ." Balorn lifted the sack and slung it over his shoulder. "I want you to bring me back some red witches alive." He lifted a hand to silence Renwick's protest before it began. "I know what your father wants, and I don't care. It will be easier to experiment with them alive. Hennen's plotting to exterminate the red coven has gone too well, and until we can find the last High Mountain royals, we have no way to use the Immortal Blade."

"I will do my best, Uncle," he replied, staring at the round outlines in the putrid bag.

"That sword is the key to everything." Balorn tipped his chin to the doorway. "Come, Witchslayer, we have work to do."

# CHAPTER FIVE

R enwick had one obligatory engagement on this trip that he had dreaded almost more than the blue witch fortress—dinner with the Lord of Murreneir. The Lord's manor was unlike the castles and temples in the other parts of the Northern Court. Instead of stone spires, it was made of redwood, like the rest of the town, albeit to a much grander scale. The enormous manor took up an entire city block. Huge two-story windows were filled with golden light, beckoning passersby to admire the decorations of boughs of pine. Garlands of dried lemon hung across the frames, and crystals dangled, catching the light of the crimson candles below. A festive feast for the eyes, soon the manor would be covered in rambling roses and soft spring-time colors.

Staff had swiftly begun placing back out the garden arch-ways and wooden benches that had wintered inside the manor when the whole town was buried under snow. There were no iron gates, no tall fencing separating the manor from the rest of the town. The gardens were treated as a community space, families picnicking on the lawns and chil-dren playing under the willow tree. His father said the fae of Murreneir were too soft-hearted, their Lord too lenient, and that he should have known Renwick's mother would be the same. For his mother was the only child of Slava Berecraft, Lord of Murreneir.

Renwick hated the stilted conversations at the dinner table between his grandfather and himself. Lord Berecraft invited Balorn to dine with them, but it was clearly a relief to both of them that Balorn had not attended.

They retired into his grandfather's study for drinks, another custom that Renwick was obliged to uphold. At least he could focus on the liquor in his hand—a traditional aniseed drink, spicy with hints of licorice. It warmed the body and quieted the mind.

Berecraft walked down the towering shelves of books, holding his glass of amber liquid. "I have more books than I shall ever read," he mused, breaking the ice.

Renwick frowned at the tray of powdered desserts set upon the low table. "At least you have time to read them . . . Murreneir seems to run itself these days."

His grandfather huffed. "Just because I don't seem panicked doesn't mean I'm not busy." He pulled back the red velvet curtain insulating the room from the cold windowpane, peering out onto the shadowed gardens. "The migration back to the town always has its bumps. The heavy snows leave damage, and not everyone has the means to fix it. The community must work together to help bring Murreneir back to life each spring."

Renwick leaned onto the arm of his leather chair, resting his chin on his fist. "Have you assembled a point man to oversee the renovations?"

Berecraft grunted from the rim of his glass, swallowing his drink to say, "Yes. And we will be experimenting with the dining halls this year too. I should think that will provide some much-needed relief as well."

"Dining halls?" Renwick furrowed his brow. "Like you do on the ice lakes? I thought that was merely a necessity of the ice camps?"

"It is," Berecraft said. "Most families don't have cooking facilities on the ice, so we have communal dining, but there are other benefits to such a system too." He traced his fingers along the dusty spines of his books and moved to a framed city map mounted to the wall. "Some return to Murreneir with broken chimneys or more work in the day with no time to cook." He pointed to four spots on the map. "At lunchtime each day, when the twelfth bell tolls, the dining commons will open to all citizens to eat."

"And who will cook this food?"

"I will send one of my green witches to supervise each of the four locations, but it will be the people who take turns cooking just as they do on the ice lakes." Berecraft smiled sadly at the map. "Not all of us have big families to dine with," he murmured. "I think we all miss the community of the basin when we return to Murreneir."

"It's a good idea," Renwick conceded.

"It was your mother's idea," the elderly fae murmured. "I should have listened to her and done it many years ago."

Stilling, Renwick considered his grandfather—a widower, his only daughter having passed as well. The caved-in roofs and broken chimneys were more easily fixed than the loneliness of having no one at your table. It seemed like an idea his mother would have had, from what little he knew of her. She'd seemed lovely and warm, flighty perhaps, but kind. It was so at odds with the distance she'd kept from him. They'd been close when he was young. He had distant memories of them laughing together, but that was far in the past now. The last handful of years, she'd been utterly vacant, most of Eadwin's life. He hated her for it, and yet, he understood it too. This life would break even the brightest shining light.

Clearing his throat, Renwick diverted the conversation. "I have visited your brown witch apothecary in town. It surprises me you allow her to run her own shop."

Berecraft turned, silver eyebrow arching. "I'm not the only one who is lenient with my witches."

Renwick knew he spoke of Aneryn. The girl was quiet but brave, steely but bold and unbroken. He had promised her mother that he would protect her, and it was the first vow he intended on upholding.

"Witches were once our prophets, and now they are our property," Berecraft muttered, finishing the glass in his hand and glowering at Renwick. "Only those fearful of losing power make such desperate grabs to obtain it. Instead of elevating himself with his leadership, your father has stepped upon others to make himself seem taller."

"You could be killed for saying such things," Renwick warned. The wine at dinner mixed with the brandy had clearly loosened his tongue.

"And what could they possibly take from me that I haven't already lost?"

Berecraft stared at him, eyes hollow with an edged sadness. "They could take your home and your title before they take your life. There are plenty of my father's friends waiting for a Lordship of their own."

The words landed like a punch to his gut. He scanned his grandfather up and down, watching his pale blue eyes narrow. How many rulers charged with protecting their people only thought of the consequences to themselves? "My father would make certain you knew all the ways you failed your people before you died."

"You will make a good King, Renwick," Berecraft murmured, rubbing his hand thoughtfully across his jaw.

Renwick didn't reply, turning to gaze into the fire.

Sighing, Berecraft walked to the bookshelf, selecting a tome. "You and I were never particularly close. Your father kept you away from me for most of your youth, though your mother tried to bring you here whenever occasion allowed."

"I have no memory of that," he gritted out.

Berecraft's voice dropped to a whisper. "I don't think Hennen liked my influence. The ways of Murreneir are different than Drunehan." He turned the book over in his

32

hand, smoothing down the dusty leather. "They say it was a sickness that took your mother and brother . . ."

Chest constricting, Renwick straightened, clasping his hands together. It was the same story he was told as well. The world only knew that the Queen and young Prince died, a mysterious illness claiming them. But anyone who knew the Vostemurs wouldn't believe the tale. Not one servant could attest to caring for them, not a single person saw their bodies, and yet the fae were too afraid to ask.

"A *sickness* that the most powerful King in Okrith with the most powerful witches and healers couldn't See coming, nor heal," Berecraft hissed, his grip on calm loosened. His eyes scanned the shelves as if trying to make sense of it all.

"It doesn't matter," Renwick growled. "They're gone, Berecraft. Let it go."

"Let it go?" he bellowed. Berecraft clenched his jaw, seemingly trying to regain control of his temper.

The normally jovial Lord of Murreneir was just as broken beneath his layers of finery. None of them had survived these years unharmed.

"I'm sorry. I wish I could explain myself, but I can't." Turning, he passed Renwick the book in his hand. "I know you and your mother weren't close in your later years. She stayed here with Eadwin to . . . keep him safe. Your brother was a lot like your mother in ways that I cannot explain."

Renwick huffed bitterly as he stared down at the book: *Songs of Spring in Murreneir*. "Perhaps I am more like my mother than any of you realized." Berecraft's eyebrows shot up, his mouth going slack as he shook his head. "Perhaps I simply hide it better because I'm determined to survive."

His heart hardened at that surprised look. No one had suspected—no one had considered him at all. His mother left him behind, the whole Berecraft side of his family distancing themselves to protect his mother and little brother. Only now that they were gone did Lord Berecraft suddenly want to rekindle these familial bonds.

Setting the book down, leaving it unopened, Renwick stood. Smoothing his hands down his trouser legs, he said, "It is getting late, I think I shall retire."

"Ren—"

"Goodnight, Lord Berecraft," Renwick dismissed, leaving without looking back. His grandfather had considered the need of an entire city—had worried for the loneliness of an entire population—and hadn't even considered that of his grandson. Renwick scowled. Hennen Vostemur was a cold-hearted ruler, but at least he didn't pretend he was anything else. There was no world in which Renwick belonged . . . the only way to have one would be to make it himself.

# CHAPTER SIX

Wavy brown hair whipped in the wind as a young fae battled a red witch for control of his dagger. She had warm brown skin a shade lighter than Aneryn's, with freckles across the bridge of her nose. Renwick's heart seized as the fae screamed, finally gaining a hand on the dagger and driving it into the boy's chest. He watched her, wide-eyed, as blood began burbling from his mouth. Renwick tried to call to the girl, but nothing came out. Her head twisted toward the dense forest beyond as shouting male voices echoed around her.

"Run!" Renwick yelled at her, a fear gripping him like one he had never known before.

The girl glanced over her shoulder, and for a moment, he swore she was looking straight at him. And then she fled, scattering like a startled deer back into the forest just before three gruff fae burst through the woods. Black sacks tied to their belts, swords already unsheathed—witch hunters. But why was a fae girl running from witch hunters?

The world spun in shades of blue and violet, his body buzzing as the mist cleared in his mind's eye. A red witch knelt in a pool of blood, a Northern guard readying to strike with his long sword. Screams and sobs echoed around the great hall of Drunehan as the earth shook. Before his dream could capture her face, it shifted to the scent of wildflowers and fresh spring rain. A smooth, warm body pressed against his as soft linens brushed against his bare skin. A hand stroked down his cheek as lush lips pressed to his, her breath tasting like cinnamon tea. Eyes shut, Renwick snaked his hand around the curvy body and hauled her tighter against him. It was a practiced movement, one his muscles had seemed to have done hundreds of times before.

"We have to wake up," that raspy feminine voice murmured.

Renwick groaned. "I just fell asleep."

He felt her chuckle through his entire body, the sweetest sound. Somehow he knew it was hard-won.

Lips pressed to the shell of his ear, the brush of her breath making his whole body tingle. "You've got to marry me today."

Tightening his arms around her, a grin stretched across his face. The feeling in the center of his chest was so unfamiliar. It didn't just feel light, it felt like a bright glowing beam of sunshine. It was joy.

Playfully nudging his nose with her own, that feminine voice whispered, "Open your eyes."

Renwick obeyed her command, opening his eyes to a cold, dark room.

He bolted up, scanning the room for the voice he had heard as readily as his own beating heart. He looked down at his hands fisted in his crumpled sheets. He blinked harder, unsure if he had just imagined the faint flicker of blue encircling his fingertips.

Panting, he threw his legs out of bed and buried his head in his hands. He was losing his mind, his grip on reality slipping from his fingers, stuck forever in the moment before it shattered.

He needed to find the brown witch apothecary, see if she could help. As he tugged on his tunic and boots from beside his bed, Thador entered.

"Nightmares?" he asked, shutting the door behind him and leaning against the wall.

"Something like that," Renwick growled, grabbing his flask from his bedside table. "I need to go to the apothecary to refill this."

"It's not dawn yet," Thador said.

Rubbing his forehead, Renwick grumbled, "It will be soon."

The soldier nodded, pushing off the doorframe. "I'll go get ready."

"I can go on my—"

"I'm your personal guard," Thador asserted, having given this speech to Renwick many times before. "There's still drunks and scoundrels roaming the streets this time of morning. I'll wait at the front of the shop, but I'm coming."

Renwick scowled. "Fine."

They left Aneryn asleep on the couch; she had left her room down the hall in the night again to sleep closer to them. He knew what it felt like—waiting to be attacked from all sides. He had promised Aneryn's mother that he'd look out for her, and he worried every day that he would break that promise.

As they ambled down the quiet streets of Murreneir, the heavy blanket of clouds parted, yielding to beams of bright morning sunlight. Winter was easing its grip on the town. Murreneir was a stunning city filled with redwood buildings and golden thatched roofs. Sleds pulled by winter oxen ferried goods from the campsite on the ice lakes, their wooden bellies scraping along the slick ice roads. Soon the ice would melt and the oxen would go to pasture, replaced by the wintering horses and carriages. The changes in the seasons was evident all around them, from shop owners painting their windowsills to the groaning cracks of ice melting in Lyrei Basin. Soon the whole town would smell of wildflowers and fresh spring rains . . . a scent branded on his soul. That's what she smelled like—his dream siren—like Murreneir in springtime.

Down the path of muddied snow was a rundown shop. The paint had flaked completely off the apothecary's sign, leaving only splintering wood. Though the sign on the door read CLOSED, it opened when Renwick tested it. Thador waited outside, toeing the snow with his boot.

"Be with you in a minute," a high voice called from the back room.

"Take your time, Evie," Renwick called as the bells on the door jangled behind him.

"Oh, it's you," she muttered.

Renwick chortled; he wasn't used to such a reception. Evelyn Doledir was certainly the most brash brown witch he had ever met.

Evie entered, carrying a wicker basket of dried sage. "You're back sooner than I anticipated. You need more?" she asked, nodding to the flask in Renwick's hand. Setting the basket on the countertop, she brushed a wisp of her auburn hair off her face.

"Yes," Renwick said tightly, placing the flask down in front of her.

She tugged on her leather collar as if it had suddenly tightened. The crest of the Lord of Murreneir was etched into the stone tag, denoting she was his property. The Lord was more lenient than most with his witches. He allowed Evie to still run her shop since it benefitted his city, which, in turn, benefitted him. More witches were being sold to the Northern Court, caught up in the skirmishes on the borders. There wasn't as much money in them as red witch heads, but it kept the witch hunters busy while they searched for the last of the red coven. Evie's Western accent gave her away. She was not raised in the North.

She pulled out a basket of brown glass vials from behind her desk. Uncorking them one at a time, she poured them into the mouth of his flask. The sleep potion was meant to be diluted in water, but for Renwick's purposes he needed it full strength. It had to be quick. The potion was suspended in alcohol, giving it the common scent of liquor, perfect for being undetected. But every time he went into the blue witch fortress, he feared that his uncle would ask for a swig. If Balorn knew, he'd kill him. It wasn't a guess; it was a certainty. His father might mourn him for a day before finding another wife to sire more heirs.

"It's been working well for you?" she asked, breaking the stilted silence.

Renwick nodded. He didn't know what it was about Evie —she spoke to him with such familiarity, as a sibling might, despite her position in life. He supposed it came with the territory; apothecaries treated more than physical maladies, they diagnosed illnesses of the mind as well. They kept the secrets of whole cities. But Evie didn't have a gentle, motherly bone in her body like most of the healers he knew. She was gruff and brutally honest, but also didn't judge—a skill which would make her clients able to reveal all sorts of embarrassing afflictions.

"You will make a better ruler than your father." She said it as if she couldn't be killed just for uttering the words.

He hated when people told him that. It felt like another crushing weight—to be mounded with their hopes that he wouldn't be as evil as his father. Others praised him for his coldheartedness, their expectations pulling him in the opposite direction to be more like his father. He couldn't be everything to everyone; at some point he would have to choose.

"I am just as evil as the rest of them. I torture witches too," Renwick snarled. "I'm just too much of a coward to look them in the eyes while I do it."

"I don't think the witches would see it that way." She

huffed, pouring the last vial into the flask and sealing the lid. "If you're ever about to torture me, please by all means, do the cowardly thing so that I don't have to be awake for it."

Renwick scowled down at the flask. The only thing that separated him from the rest of his family was that his actions pained him. He wondered how many more years it would take of being called Witchslayer before he embodied that moniker. When the whole world treated him like a monster, he was doomed to become one.

A blinding pain shot behind his eyes, and he rubbed a hand to his temples, screwing his eyelids shut. He pushed down harder on the feeling rising within him, an undeniable urge bursting into his being. Flashes of freckles and smiling lips, wildflowers and rain. He clenched his jaw tighter, holding his breath until the rising wave ebbed.

Evie busied herself setting aside the empty vials, though she clearly noted his episode.

"Do you have anything for headaches?" he growled.

She did not look up from her ledger as she said, "Not that kind of headache."

The room was silent as he stared at her, unspoken secrets floating between them. Renwick produced a gold coin from his pocket and set it on her ledger. "For the flask," he said, then set another two gold coins beside it. "And for your silence."

"I'm an apothecary. Secrets are part of the profession," she said, taking the coins, her hazel eyes meeting his. "And now that I have the coin for it"—she waggled her eyebrows— "How about a drink? Perhaps it will help with the headaches."

"It's barely dawn. That sounds like a terrible idea," Renwick replied. "People will talk."

"*Fae* will talk," she countered. "But I'm talking about the humans' gambling hall. A place I can't get into without my Lord's permission . . . and seeing as you are the Lord of my Lord . . ."

Renwick chuckled. He liked this brown witch. Rubbing his thumb down his forefinger, he murmured, "Gambling, you say?" His lips twisted up. "I suppose I have time for one hand before the day begins."

# CHAPTER SEVEN

The Forbidden Thistle Tavern was nothing like the castles he was accustomed to, and Renwick loved it. No gilded mirrors or opulent candelabras—here, there were simple furnishings, functional though unfashionable. The humans crowded around the seedy space, cards strewn across the table as they played two kings. The pleasant hum of liquor coursed through his body as Renwick examined his cards.

"You bring the strangest sort here, Evie," the player across from them said, sliding his gaze to the brown witch. "You in or out?"

"Whatever it takes to be granted entry. Besides, you don't mind when the strange sort has pocketfuls of coins, do you, Lawrence?" The brown witch tossed in her cards with a muttered curse, making the other players chuckle.

It was hard finding gambling halls where his title didn't put people off. Only the most sordid locations would do. Evie had brought him through a labyrinth of back alleyways to arrive at this tavern, where the patrons looked like scoundrels and did not care one lick that he was a prince so long as he could pay his debts at the end of the night. Thador sat scowling into his glass of ale at the bar, clearly unhappy with this change of plans but unable to say so.

"Aye, especially now that His Majesty has canceled the build of the Spring Castle," the smaller man, Lawrence, grumbled, wiping a sweaty hand across his brow. His cold blue eyes stared at Renwick. "I suppose he doesn't have need of a castle for his Queen anymore." Renwick peered back, equally unfeeling. "The least he could do is pay us to build a memorial or something. I've got a whole crew out of work."

Renwick shrugged, focusing back on his cards rather than responding to Lawrence's complaints. He heard from jilted people all the time. The gambling halls were filled with the unlucky underbelly of society, the ones who slipped through the cracks, and his father did nothing to save them. They spoke to Renwick as if he had any sway over his father, as if he too weren't someone slipping through the cracks.

He wouldn't be surprised if they tried to mob him. But they were mostly human here in these taverns; the elegant inn he was staying in was reserved for fae. Thador could take them all singlehandedly. His guard was always chastising him from coming to these places. It was a good thing they were returning to the Southern Court, where you could throw a stone and hit a card game.

Renwick laid down a queen, waiting for the human across from him.

The man guffawed, throwing in his cards and looking to the gruff bear of a man beside him. The man put down a king, and it was Renwick's turn to grimace. He put down a seven of the same suit and prayed the man did not have a higher card. When the man put down a queen, the muscle in Renwick's cheek twitched with restraint, trying not to show his disappointment.

"Ha!" the man snickered, hauling his coins back to his side of the table. Lawrence took a long drink from his tankard as his belly shook with laughter.

"One more hand, and then I better be going," Evie said,

casting a sidelong glare at Renwick as if to say he should do the same. As the men across from them got lost more in the drink, the game would become more volatile and he would have to move on. The windowless room gave no sign of the time, but it had to be mid-morning. He should be riding out to the blue witch fortress by now.

It was a minor release, these games he played, something to distract him from the bigger woes of the world. Cards took a level of focus that quieted the rest of the noises shouting in his mind. It was a mixture of cunning and luck, like everything in life, some days being dealt better cards than others.

"Why aren't you up at the Lord's manor, Your Highness?" Lawrence asked. "Not fond of your grandpapa?"

The nameless man beside him chortled. "The tiresome life of fine linens and crystal goblets."

Renwick frowned. He knew it made him seem ungrateful. The finery was all a beautiful facade, but there was no denying that full bellies were better than empty ones and warm clothes better than threadbare. Still, it was a cell like any other, and he'd much rather the warmth of a small room and greasy tavern food than the chill of cold stone castles and decadent fare. He knew he should be grateful—he'd been *told* he should be grateful his whole life—but whenever he attempted to summon the feeling, he came up lacking.

"How's your Sara doing, Lawrence?" Evie asked, redirecting the conversation. "Does she need any more settlers for her stomach?"

Lawrence's countenance changed in a flash, the lines on his face warming into a smile. "She's doing much better, Evie, now that the first few months have passed."

"You're having another one?" The man beside him laughed, clapping him on the back.

"Have I not told you?" Lawrence chuckled. "Aye, number six is on the way after all these years. I thought those days were surely behind us, what with us getting on."

The man shook his head. "I thought it would be your Tess that would be the next with child, since she's getting married this spring."

"One getting married and one on the way." Evie shook her head with a smile. "You are a lucky man, Lawrence."

A knot tightened in the center of Renwick's chest, that feeling of buzzing building within him as if it might come spilling out. He needed to get out of there, out into the cold air. The heat and scent of the tavern rose, his senses assaulted, everything suddenly too loud, too bright. Thador seemed to notice, sculling his drink and grabbing his cloak off the chair beside him.

"I'd be more lucky if I wasn't out of work." Lawrence looked to Renwick again as if it were all his fault. "Do you think the King will ever resume the build of the Spring Castle?"

Swallowing the burning knot rising up his throat, Renwick pursed his lips. "One day the castle will be built, whether it is in years or decades I cannot say . . . but I could have a small job for you." He tossed his coin pouch over to Lawrence. "Keep the site clear. Keep it ready for when the time comes. It is not that much work, but I will send money each year for the project. And in the meanwhile, the Lord of Murreneir is working on a building project of his own. Perhaps I can recommend you to him."

Lawrence's eyes widened, clearly surprised Renwick had bent to his taunting. "Th-thank you, Your Highness."

Standing, Renwick straightened his jacket, taking a deep breath to push against the buzzing inside him. "Keep the money," he said, looking at the table. "I should be going."

Evie gave him a wary look, but Renwick gave her a brief nod, and she left it. She knew what was happening to him as well as he did. Thador's hand landed hard on his shoulder, steering him out of the crowded room as his eyesight began to blur.

Renwick turned, barreling out into the street, the cold air

rushing into his lungs as the morning sun beamed above him. The roar of magic filled his ears as he stumbled into the back alleyway, away from prying eyes. A vision begged to be released. He rubbed his head, trying to push down on it harder.

Groaning, he crouched, covering his head in his hands as the searing pain tore through him.

Thador squeezed the back of his neck. "You're safe," he murmured, his voice a low rumble. "No one's here. Breathe."

His arms shook with the exertion of restraining the magic burning inside him, poisoning his veins. As his eyes clouded over, he saw her—at least, he knew it was her even from behind, her dark brown hair spilling in tight waves down her back as she crouched in front of someone. Smiling up at her was a child with a freckled nose, light brown skin, and emerald green eyes. Barking out a pained cry, the force of the vision impaled him straight through. A child.

# CHAPTER EIGHT

I t was midday before Renwick arrived for his morning shift. It had taken Thador much convincing to stay behind in Murreneir. The look of fear in his guard's eyes told him enough—he feared it would happen again in front of Balorn. They didn't speak of it, though he was certain his guard knew. Better to not discuss it even between them.

The western dormitories of the blue witch fortress were homely compared to the horrors of the main building. Grateful with every step, Renwick followed his uncle into the building. A warm hearth beckoned them into the reception hall where two soldiers stood, guarding the exit. The witches here were free to roam the building, though still under the watchful eye of the guards. They came here for the final training before they were sent off to the Lords of the Northern Court.

Through the smell of firewood and cranberries, the inky horror still leached from the black stone walls. They learned to hone their visions in the main building through pain and fear . . . but here, they learned to serve their Lords in other ways. Renwick's stomach roiled. He hated this place. Those with strong powers and beautiful faces were brought here, their training kept below the neck, their faces unscarred and their hair uncut. He didn't understand any of it, but this place he understood the least. What had any of this to do with their blue magic? He already knew the answer—nothing. It was a noxious mixture of power, lust, and cruelty.

Balorn swept past the guards and down the long corridor. Renwick followed him up to the second floor, where he stilled at a door handle, saying, "These two are being sent off to your father soon . . . Doesn't mean you can't have a little fun with them first." He looked Renwick up and down with a dissatisfied gaze. "Though it looks like you've already come straight from the brothels."

Balorn shook his head as if he were chastising a child for stealing sweets. Winking, he entered before Renwick could open his mouth to protest.

The two witches stood, their golden hair plaited down their backs. They stood as if waiting in the royal courts, hoping to snag the eye of the King. They wore sapphire blue dresses with silver filigree, surprisingly modest, covering their arms, though their bosoms were heaved up by their corsetry. Renwick wondered if they were covered to hide their scars, for there would certainly be some if they had been trained in their visions.

The room they entered was well-appointed too; clearly his uncle had been doting on these two. It held two armchairs and a lounge gathered around a low wood table atop a lush burgundy rug. Renwick assumed their bedroom was through the far door. It felt a world away from where they had just been, carving into frightened witches, and yet the twins' eyes had that same glazed-over look, like they had been tunneling so deep into themselves that only the shell remained.

The witches remained in deep bows, waiting until Balorn said, "Rise" to lift again.

When Balorn extended his hand out to one girl, she smiled and took it, perching herself on his lap as he settled into an armchair. He gestured for Renwick to do the same.

"How are my two favorite girls?" Balorn asked, sweeping the hair off the neck of the girl on his lap and tracing a finger down her collarbone. Her eyes fluttered closed as if it were pleasurable, and Renwick had to press his lips shut not to laugh.

She was doing all the right things. This was what fae males like Balorn wanted, but it made him nauseous. All he saw was a girl desperately trying to survive, so different from Tilly, a businesswoman in her power. The other witch settled on Renwick's lap the second he sat down, resting her arm around his neck, presenting her chest toward his face.

She was beautiful, but it stirred nothing within him, nor did any other person he encountered. It was just another way that he was different. All the fae around him seemed utterly consumed by desire. It was all they seemed to ever talk about, going to great lengths to constantly be easing some deep yearning. He had no idea what it was. They all seemed possessed. He tried to summon that fire, those urges, but it felt like grasping for a cloud of mist. Surely everyone around him wasn't trying so hard?

Renwick had engaged in a few trysts over the years, mostly because he felt like it was expected of him. He understood on some level that the act itself felt good, but it always left him deeply unsatisfied. No part of him yearned to repeat it. He was starting to become certain that fire didn't exist within him at all . . . and then he had his first vision of her, that first heady whiff of wildflowers and rain, and what was not even an ember within him turned into a raging fire. And he knew then that for him, the two were inseparable—he couldn't have someone's body without having their soul too.

None of the other fae seemed to have such qualms. But he only longed for someone who wasn't there—who might not even be alive at all. He wasn't sure what was worse: that he was hallucinating or that he Saw a vision of the future that would never come to pass. All he knew for certain was that he had no desire for the woman who was sitting on his knee.

His father had an entire harem to slake his desires, and Renwick did not want but one—a fae that if his father or uncle knew was alive, they would most certainly kill.

A bang on the door halted Balorn's lips skimming up the witch's neck.

"What?" he shouted.

"We're having problems with twelve again, Your Highness," a muffled voice came through the door.

Balorn snarled, shoving the witch off his lap and adjusting his trousers as he stood. "I'll return later. Make sure my nephew has some fun." He didn't look at Renwick as he left the room.

Renwick nudged the nameless witch on his knee and said, "Sit on the lounge."

"Yes, Your Highness," she muttered, hiding whatever relief she might have felt.

The two of them sat side-by-side on the lounge, looking bored rather than frightened, as though they were resigned to whatever their lives had become.

"Can you summon visions now?" he asked them.

They looked between each other, confused, and then back to him. "Yes, Your Highness."

"And do you have visions when you don't summon them?"

"Sometimes," the twin on the left hedged.

"Can you stop the visions when you don't want them?"

They narrowed their eyes at him, clearly having never been asked the question before.

"I'm trying to understand how blue witch magic works," he muttered, adding quickly, "If I can explain it better, perhaps I can prove such methods don't need to be used."

"Things were never this way because they needed to be," the one on the right murmured, pausing between each word as if assessing if she would be punished for them. "They are this way because your father and uncle want them to be."

Renwick rubbed his temples. It was true.

"We were ten when we were brought here, the same age as most witches when their powers begin to manifest," the one on the left said. "And each year, our powers grew stronger, just as your uncle's punishments grew greater, until we reached maturity and suddenly we were trained."

Renwick blinked at her. He recognized it so well: it was the look of a survivor, of someone who did whatever they had to do to hang on. How far they must have been forced to retreat in on themselves to come out the other side of this place together.

"You tell me, Witchslayer," the one on the right said, placing her tongue in her cheek. "Would we have been just as powerful if we had never come here?"

He sighed, knowing the conversation had reached a terrible end. They hid it well around Balorn, but for whatever reason, they let him know the truth under their carefree exteriors. They were all acting in whatever ways they needed.

Rubbing his forehead, he stood. "You seem prepared to survive this. You are good at hiding your weaknesses." They nodded in unison. ". . . apart from one."

The twins blanched, looking between each other. "What else could he take from us?"

Renwick's eyes guttered. "Each other." The one on the left opened her mouth to protest, but Renwick pressed on. "Hate each other. Fight each other. Injure each other if you must. Make it seem like it's a punishment to be kept together." He ambled to the door handle, looking back over his shoulder at them. "Good luck."

# CHAPTER NINE

R enwick entered the cold atrium, where Balorn was waiting for him, a piece of paper in his hands.

"Had some fun?" Balorn tipped his head to Renwick as he pulled at the belt of his trousers. He had intentionally buckled it looser upon leaving the dormitories. The lies were in the details.

"Not as much as in Ruttmore, but fine," he said with a wicked grin, shaking out his disheveled clothes.

"You are slowly building an unsavory reputation, Witch-slayer," Balorn said, eyeing his mud-stained hems. "I should like you to come to work in more presentable attire."

He huffed a cavalier laugh. "Yes, Uncle."

Balorn stepped in closer to him, as if the walls could hear. "You think your grin and steely eyes won't give you away." Renwick's heart leapt into his throat as he waited for his uncle to continue. "One look at those clothes, and everyone can see you're drowning." Balorn smoothed a hand down Renwick's rumpled tunic. "You shouldn't be mourning that bitch of a mother at all, but if you must, learn to hide it better."

Renwick swallowed the knot in his throat. "Yes, Uncle."

He hid his relief behind his hard stare. His uncle thought he was mourning his mother. He thought grief was the secret that Renwick held so tight. It was almost laughable.

"This one is a handful," Balorn said, passing him the paper. "She's holding back on her visions, I'm sure of it. Persuade her."

The number 12 was stamped on the sheet of paper with a name written across the top: Nave Mallor. Below her name was a list of her indiscretions: verbal insults, spitting on guards, biting, etc., and next to it was a list of punishments: flaying, flogging, starvation . . .

His stomach roiled, but he simply nodded to his uncle, taking the ring of keys from his outstretched hand. "I just need the rest of her notes."

"Make me proud," Balorn said, giving Renwick a wink and heading back towards his office.

Shaking out his hands, Renwick took a steeling breath and headed to the office at the top of the stairs. The scrolls sat in a basket in the corner, each with the witches' cell numbers. The collected information on each of them sat mostly untouched. They probably thought it was easier to hurt them if they didn't know their lives' stories . . . but they were wrong.

As he entered the belly of the mountain, moaning bellows echoed up the stone steps. The place was never silent, always someone shrieking or groaning, long after the guards had retired and the witches were locked in their cells. The stench would stay with him as long as he lived. The fear was so palpable, it clouded the air, feeling like pinpricks from his fingertips up to the crown of his head.

Renwick's hands gripped the keyring tightly, trying to stamp on those icy raindrops pricking his hands. He slotted the key into the lock, wishing desperately he could turn back but knowing that this was the only path forward. He pushed the horror down deeper, fusing it into his own soul.

"Oh, the fearsome Witchslayer," the singsong voice from the day earlier echoed out to him.

Nave Mallor was still strung up by her wrists, her face and arms covered in bruises and her long silver hair spilling over her shoulders. Dark sunken in eyes glared out at him. Practically a corpse, clearly she had gone too many days without food or water.

"You're holding back your visions?" Renwick asked by way of greeting. He entered the room, shutting the door and leaning against it.

Nave tried to spit at him, but it didn't reach him across the cell.

"I don't answer to you," she snarled.

"I'm afraid you do," he countered, pulling out his dagger with his free hand.

Nave didn't so much as flinch.

"Why are you fae so obsessed with your futures?" Nave scowled as she tugged on her restraints. "Perhaps you can avoid a battle here and there, but the Goddess of Death will call your name all the same."

"Those who know the future will be the strongest of any court."

"Do you feel strong, Witchslayer?" Nave looked him up and down, eyes tracking the same disheveled attire that his uncle had noted before. "All I see is weakness."

Renwick pushed off the wall, his dagger tip pressing against her neck in a split second. "Keep talking like that, and all you will See of my future is me killing you."

Nave's lips twisted up into a sinister smirk. "I welcome death."

He huffed, stepping away. He scrunched up his tunic sleeves as if preparing for a mess as he passed the scroll from hand to hand. Nave merely grinned.

"So you welcome death," he murmured, scanning her from her matted head to her cracked and bleeding feet. "You do not fear hunger or pain?"

"No." She smiled from yellowing cracked teeth. "You cannot break me."

"You're wrong," he said, opening the scroll. "Nave Mallor of Eastport, daughter of Betris and Ean Mallor, property of Lord Tumner. One younger sister, Onyx." He peered up at her from the paper, and her sneering mask slipped for a split second.

There.

"She doesn't have any magic." Her words came out very carefully, a calculated, neutral tone so unlike the feral snarling from a moment before. "You can ask Lord Tumner yourself. She is useless as a witch, better as a maid."

Renwick glanced down at the scroll. "She's twelve, her visions might still be developing."

"They aren't," Nave gritted out.

Cocking his eyebrow, Renwick pursed his lips. "I'm sure the guards would be up for a challenge."

"I wouldn't do that, Witchslayer," Nave growled. "Don't threaten my family."

He rolled the scroll and dropped it to the floor. "I won't if you behave."

Nave leaned forward, straining against her chains. "Do you want me to tell you your future, Witchslayer? For I have tried, and when it comes to you, I haven't Seen anything at all."

His ears rang, the sounds of the fortress muffled by the rushing of his blood. Acid burned its way up his throat as he stared into Nave's dark eyes, his world crashing down upon him. Her lip curled as she watched her blow land.

In a blink, he had his dagger at her throat again. Baring his teeth, he warned, "Silence."

"I went searching in my mind's eye for the future of another though," Nave whispered, eyes staring deep into his soul. "Do you See her too? This freckles and wildflowers girl?" Beads of blood pooled at Nave's neck from the dagger, but she continued, her grin widening. "Do you know who she is? *What* she is?"

"Stop."

"F—"

The dagger plunged deep into her neck, silencing her words. Her eyes bulged as she gurgled and choked on the viscous scarlet liquid. She smiled at him one more time, trails of foaming blood dripping from her mouth, and then her body went limp.

Renwick stood there frozen, hands trembling and his heart pounding through his ribcage. That was too close . . . far too close. His life would have imploded around him with one more whispered word. She welcomed death, he tried to comfort himself with that notion, but it did nothing to lessen the cold sting of the truth that he was the one to deliver her to it.

He pulled his dagger from her lifeless body, a pool of blood stretching out from below her. His heart thundered in his chest.

"What is this?" a voice snarled from behind him.

Renwick spun, finding Balorn looming in the doorway. Every muscle in his body tensed as he wondered how long his uncle had been standing there.

Balorn strode into the cell, lifting Nave's head by her hair to look into her lifeless eyes. "She was one of our most promising witches, her gift of Sight unparalleled. You weren't meant to kill her."

"I was just trying to draw her out," Renwick hedged. "I didn't mean it to be fatal."

"You didn't expect a dagger to the throat to be fatal?" Balorn whirled on him, eyes filled with fire.

Renwick shrugged, trying to brush it off as incompetence as his uncle loomed over him. "I just got carried away."

"Hmm." A blinding pain shot through Renwick's thigh, and he looked down to see his uncle's dagger plunged into his leg. "Next time, stab them here." He withdrew his dagger and stabbed it back into Renwick's arm. "Or here. Or better yet, some long thin slices that open every time you breathe." A gasping scream escaped from Renwick's mouth as his uncle raked the dagger across his ribs, shredding his clothes to scraps. "Only go for the throat when you want to make it quick. Be grateful I granted your mother and brother that blessing."

Renwick's eyes flared, staring into his uncle's heartless gaze. His confession was more painful than the weeping wounds trailing rivulets of blood down his body. Somewhere deep in his bones, he knew it was Balorn who had killed his mother and brother. Only Balorn wouldn't hesitate to kill a Queen.

Renwick tried to take a breath, but the attempt shot bolts of pain across his torso. Voice trembling, he managed to say, "Yes, Uncle."

"Good." Balorn sneered, revealing the beast that lurked beneath his mask. "You are dismissed. Ride back to Murreneir. I won't let the brown witches heal you here. Every movement of your horse will be like a fresh stab and remind you of the weight of who you are." He gripped Renwick by the tunic and shook him, slamming him back again into the stone wall. "You are the future King. Do better if you intend to survive."

Renwick stumbled forward as Balorn released him, his boots filling with blood.

"Yes, Uncle," he said, retreating to the doorway on shaky legs. He was the heir to the Northern Court, and yet he knew his father would not lift a hand to stop Balorn from killing him. There would be no punishment for this mutilation.

Renwick cringed with each step up the stairs. The Vostemur crimes were already so many, he doubted he would know forgiveness within his lifetime. He glanced at the bloody dagger sheathed at his hip. He acted like he was so different from his father and uncle, but he killed just as they did. It did not matter if his heart ached with every slice of his blade—he was a killer just like them—and he knew he would have to kill again to keep his secrets. How many more witches would die by his hand? How far was he willing to go to protect someone whom he didn't even know?

# CHAPTER TEN

If the blood loss didn't kill him, the cold might. Each step on the long walk down from the cliffs to the stables left a trail of crimson snow. The chill seeped into his damp clothes as fresh warm blood dripped down his body. The coppery tang filled his nostrils. It was too much blood, even for a fae, and he began to wonder if his uncle had never intended for him to survive.

He wrapped his wounds as best he could. Discarding his weapons in his cloak pockets, he bound the sodden fabric with his belts. Balorn had been right: each gallop of his horse made him gasp in pain, the wounds pulling open during the torturous ride back to Murreneir. Every time the bleeding seemed to stop, his wounds would tear again, but he knew he must make haste. Slowing his horse for a less painful ride would leave him dead in the snow. He needed to find Evie. She would be able to heal him.

Murreneir had never felt so far, the short ride seeming to stretch out for hours. As the frosty air froze his clothes, a blanket of warmth descended over him like sinking into a hot bath. He battled against the sensation, trying not to slip under that warm water, desperately clinging onto the pain that shot through him.

As spots clouded his vision, his grip on the reins loosened. His horse navigated the thin trails without guidance, maintaining her urgent gallop. Down and down to the valley where Murreneir sat nestled between two looming hills, he prayed to all the Gods to hang on for one moment longer.

Eyes clouding over, he stared through space and time to a rooftop dusted in snow. Reality warped as a warm back pressed against his chest. He wrapped his arms around her, staring out over a sleepy village.

A shooting pain lanced through his side, and he gritted his teeth, trying to hold onto that image. He filled his body with the feel of her soft skin and the scent of her hair. A faraway voice echoed around him as he gripped tighter to that vision. *Stay with me, hold onto me*, he begged her through the dark corners of his mind even as his body went limp.

*I see you.* Her voice was the warmth of spring sunlight, the hushed tone of late nights and whispered confessions. The sound filled every crack inside of him as he let go of the world and moved only toward her.

The hard smack of the ground pulled him back into his body, his waking dream washing away to the utter agony of his wounds. His shoulder throbbed but protected his head from cracking against the stone. No longer able to separate his injuries, his whole body begged for relief.

Looking around him, he blinked away his vision. He was in a back alley in Murreneir, Evie's apothecary shop two doors down. He glanced at his horse. They had made it somehow. Hands biting against the frozen ground, he pushed himself up and saw a man watching him from a stoop.

"Your Highness . . ." His face drained of blood as he gaped at Renwick, pointing a trembling finger at him. "Y-your eyes."

Renwick spat a splatter of blood on the cobblestones, glaring at his flickering blue fingertips as he rose on swaying feet. "Stop," he commanded, trying to silence the man before he drew any more spectators. He wobbled like a fawn over to the stunned man, slinging his arm over the man's shoulder, unable to hold himself up.

The man tried to push away. "You're . . . You're a—"

Before he could finish the thought, Renwick's dagger was in his gut. The man's hazel eyes bugged before rolling back in his head. His body flopped like cutting a puppet's strings, twitching and spasming as he gasped his last breaths. Renwick tripped forward into the wall, having cut down the support of the man now dead at his feet.

Heaving the contents of his stomach, blood and bile splattered onto the muddy snow. He stumbled frantically away from the body and weaved toward the apothecary door. He barely made it over the threshold before he collapsed onto the floor. His shoulder didn't save him this time. His head smacked hard against the wooden slats, bringing him back from the precipice of unconsciousness.

"Mother Moon!" A gasp rang out from across the room.

Evie ran past him, locking the front door and yanking closed the blinds at the front of her shop. Her footsteps echoed across the small room as she darted to the table laden with elixirs.

"Make it stop," Renwick groaned, clenching his eyes shut and fisting his hands in his eye sockets. He curled into a ball, trying to push down on the magic erupting out of him. "They will kill me . . ."

"They already nearly have," Evie muttered, the sound of glass clinking behind her as she rushed to his side.

Flipping him onto his back, she ripped open his shirt and cursed. She unbuckled his wrapped injuries, hastily smearing a thick, stinging salve into his wounds.

"The cuts will heal, Evie," Renwick gritted out. "I need you to make this stop."

He opened his eyes to her again, seeing the shimmering sapphire in his eyes reflecting back in her own. Her hands kept applying the acrid balm, even as her gaze filled with fear.

"There might be something," she hedged, her brows knitting in concern.

"Whatever it takes, please," Renwick urged, his body trembling as the shock began to take hold of his muscles. The pressure of pushing down on the magic made his stomach rebel again, and he turned to heave more bloody bile onto the floor.

Evie didn't so much as flinch, used to all manner of maladies. "It's dangerous," she warned.

"I don't care," Renwick hissed, spitting the vile taste from his mouth. "Kill me or help me. Just don't leave me like this."

Evie scowled but got up, running behind the counter and coming back with a vial. "Just a sip," she instructed, dripping the bitter fluid into his mouth.

Acid burned down his throat as he grimaced against the overwhelming flavor. He waited for a breath, praying to every God, before a warm tingling began coursing below his skin. The sensation spread, numbing his fingers and toes. His mouth went slack and his breathing steadied as that golden warmth caressed his skin. Sighing, his eyes fluttered closed for a moment, basking in the glorious quiet of his mind.

"Moon's blessing," Evie whispered. "It worked."

Renwick peered to his warming fingertips as the glow disappeared. He touched his fingertips to his thumb. He couldn't feel them anymore, beautifully numbed, the magic within them snuffed out.

"What is this magic tonic?" He rubbed a hand down his face, leaving little bubbly echoes in the wake of his touch.

"It is a family recipe," Evie whispered, corking the bottle. "My great-great-grandmother's. She was a violet witch, if my mother is to be believed, though anyone I could ask is long gone."

She began to put the vial in the pocket of her apron when Renwick reached out and grabbed her wrist. Her shape was a blur. He blinked but was unable to focus his eyes, though he couldn't summon an ounce of panic within him. He had never felt more calm.

"I'm going to need that bottle," he murmured. "And any more that you have."

"This potion is meant to aid the dying, to ease their transition into the afterlife," Evie warned. "It is not some sleeping elixir like what is in your flask. It will sooner kill you than save you."

"I will be killed without it," he murmured, the pain having ebbed enough for him to finally face what had just happened.

He had killed two people in only a matter of hours. Were it not for the threats of Nave Mallor, he probably would've let it consume him, slipping into the undertow of his pain. But his life wasn't only his own and, while he had been resigned to his own doomed fate, he couldn't bear to doom her as well.

Keeping a gentle grip on her wrist, his eyes welled. The panic gave way to the horrible truth—he had to survive this. Perhaps those visions were tricks of his mind sent to taunt him, a future that would never be. No, he felt it in every cell of his body. She was alive. He did not know if they'd ever get to that snow-covered rooftop, the vision that had saved him, but he couldn't give up when her life was at stake. He cared more for the fate of this stranger than he had ever cared for himself.

"I have two bottles," Evie relented, passing him the vial. Her expression pinched as she scanned his face. "You'll have to come back for more when you run out. Take it sparingly, only when you are truly desperate," she warned.

Renwick closed his fingers around the vial. "Thank you, Evie."

"I may be the only person alive who still knows how to make it." Her voice tinged with sorrow before she cleared her throat, brushing off whatever memory plagued her. "I wouldn't tell anyone anyway, but that fact alone should keep you from killing me for knowing your secret."

Renwick's head dropped back in relief, though he misjudged, smacking it against the floor. He couldn't feel the thud of his skull colliding with the wood.

Evie hissed at him. "Lie still," she ordered. "I will find someone to fetch your guard, and then we'll get you cleaned up."

Renwick grabbed her hand again as she stood. "When you go out the door, don't look to your left."

"I am more familiar with death than you will ever know." Her eyes saddened as she rose. "Sometimes in this life, you must choose between being a good person and being a survivor . . . and I chose to survive."

His cheeks flushed as he swallowed a lump in his throat and nodded at her. He had struggled so long to be both. Hundreds of choices he could have made differently on the twisted road that led him here. Those sweet visions haunted him, pushing him forward. As he watched Evie rush out the front door, he knew it was time to make that choice.

# CHAPTER ELEVEN

All he felt was pain as he blinked against the firelight. Nighttime had descended, the curtains drawn over darkened windows.

"Thank the fucking Gods," Thador growled, pacing in front of the hearth.

Renwick scanned the bedroom. He was back at the inn. Thador must have carried him. He couldn't remember anything more than Evie's harsh face as she left her shop. Craning his neck up, he spotted Aneryn by the doorway, picking nervously at her fingernails.

Groaning, he propped himself up on his elbows and surveyed his bandaged chest and bicep. Minty salves stained the strips of linen a pale green. Each breath stung, but the pain had lessened. His head throbbed worse than any hangover, and in his chest, he ached to feel the lightness that he had fallen asleep with. Searching the room, he found his bloodied clothes discarded over the back of a chair. The elixir Evie gave him would be in it.

Thador followed his line of sight. "She said to only take it if you can't cope without."

Aneryn grabbed a glass from the mantle, the water tinged a reddish hue. "Here," she said. "This will ease the pain. It's a good thing we're heading south. A few weeks in the salty waves of Silver Sands and you'll be fine."

Renwick huffed around the rim of his glass. She said it as if his wounds were no more than a paper cut. The cool liquid soothed his scratchy throat, leaving a sweet floral aftertaste. Something Evie left them with to lessen the inflammation, he presumed.

"I don't suppose I need to ask who did this?" Thador snarled, continuing to pace back and forth like a trapped wildcat.

"No," Renwick murmured, taking another sip as Aneryn returned to her position by the door.

"I'm going to kill him," Thador seethed, grabbing his cloak.

Renwick opened his mouth to protest as Aneryn side-stepped his guard.

"No, you're not," she said, crossing her arms as her small body blocked his path.

"Someone has to end him," Thador said, looking back at Renwick.

Aneryn cocked her head at the lumbering guard. "If you storm the blue witch fortress, you will only get yourself killed."

"So long as Balorn dies," Thador said, clasping his cloak around his neck.

"And what about me?" Aneryn didn't budge, pinning him to the spot with her glare despite being a third his size. "Who will protect me when you're gone?"

Thador's fingers stilled on the clasp. He frowned down at her and removed his cloak, chucking it on top of Renwick's bloody garments. "You had to go and say that."

Aneryn smirked. "Because it always works."

The guard chuckled, falling into the empty seat beside the pile of clothes. Cheeks dimpling, Aneryn leaned against the doorframe, victorious. She was the smallest and wisest of their trio, always saving them from themselves. It was

74

too much, a role she should have never had to play, and Renwick wondered if she'd ever have a life outside of this. He hoped one day she'd be free of him, that she could carve out her own path in the world. But in order to do that, he needed to keep going. Too many people depended on him, those in front of him and those in his mind. He clung to life by his fingernails, and even then it didn't feel like enough.

"I want you to take my entire wardrobe to the wash-woman," Renwick said, dropping his head into his hands.

Thador quirked a brow at him. "Why?"

"It is time I acted like a Prince," Renwick murmured, surveying the dried blood beneath his fingernails. "And have the maids run me a bath."

"Are you sure you don't want to rest tonight?" Aneryn asked, eyeing his bandaged chest. "You can bathe in the morning."

"We're leaving in the morning—"

"You can't ride like this," Thador said, waving a hand at him.

"Then we will take a carriage," Renwick gritted out. "I want to be out of this place before the sun is high in the sky."

"I don't blame you for that," Thador murmured, steepling his fingers in thought. "We can make it happen."

He gave a nod, bundling the pile of clothing in his burly arms, carefully patting the outline of the vial in the front pocket. When he turned to leave, Aneryn made way for him this time.

"Rest," she said, looking at Renwick. "I'll wake you when the bath is ready."

She turned to leave, but Renwick halted her with a soft, "Aneryn?"

Paused, she looked back over her shoulder, waiting for him to ask his question.

"If I asked, would you lie to me?" he murmured, his heart-beat pounding in his ears. He so desperately needed something to hang onto. "Tell me you See a future worth fighting for?"

"I don't need to," Aneryn whispered, placing her hand on the doorknob. "You already See that future for yourself."

Icy droplets of spring rain pattered on the windowpane. Renwick rested back on his pillow, closing his eyes as his soul strained out of his body toward that person he held only in his mind. He let out a shuddering breath. He could feel her even now, her soft lips, her scent, her taste . . . but most of all, he felt her absence more keenly than the slashes across his chest.

Aneryn's head bobbled against Thador's shoulder as the carriage swayed. The two of them breathed heavy, sleepy breaths in unison. Only moments off the main road, they had already fallen asleep. They embarked on their long journey to Silver Sands Harbor by carriage, Renwick too wounded to ride. Evie's magic balms had worked to expedite his healing, but the jerking of the carriage was still torturous. His aching body was nothing compared to the weariness of his soul; each turn of the carriage wheel, he resigned himself more to what he must become.

Flurries of snow danced around the fogged windows. He was glad to ride south and meet the springtime; it would be hot in Silver Sands by now. He held a parcel in his hand that he had received from a harried-looking messenger boy that morning. Inside was the book he'd left at his grandfather's house and a note. Gripping the edges so tightly the note crinkled, Renwick read it again.

*I am grateful for who you are and I am sorry that I kept my distance. I thought it would protect you. I know I cannot make up*

*for lost time, but if you ever need to call upon me, however you*
*need me, I will be there for you now.*

He understood why his grandfather had kept his distance: he'd been protecting his mother and little brother from him, The Witchslayer. Berecraft had believed Renwick's well-crafted lie that he was the monster that they feared him to be. Crumpling the note in his fist, he smoothed his hand down his perfectly starched tunic. His hair was combed back, tied in a short knot at the nape of his neck, his jaw freshly-shaven. When he'd awakened in the bed at the inn, he'd known it was time to play the part.

There were four people who knew his secret, and there could be no more. Aneryn and Thador would never tell a soul. His grandfather would remain tight-lipped and largely ignored in Murreneir. Evie knew his secret but was also helping him hide it, having secured her safety by giving him a poison only she knew how to make. Even if he was able to get the recipe and spell from her, he'd have to find another brown witch to infuse it with her magic . . . too many loose ends.

He mindlessly patted the vial in his pocket. He hadn't needed it so far today. He hoped over time he would be able to go without it longer and longer, able to stamp out the magic entirely. But when the potion had worked its way out of his system, the visions burbled behind his eyelids, pain stabbing through his temple to keep them at bay. He rubbed his forehead, screwing his eyes shut and forcing the magic out of his body. Breathing, the buzzing ebbed.

Maybe the world would be righted in a year or two. Things would get better soon. Maybe he wouldn't need the elixir and could freely be who he was. His mind flashed with the image of Nave Mallor's lifeless, bloodied body. It wasn't just an impossible hope, it was also one he was unworthy of —a dream of being like the people he killed. Looking up to the flattened hilltop bare of trees, he pressed his lips together. Waiting for a castle that would never be built, the baldness of that hope was displayed for all to see.

How would the future receive him if he had to corrupt his soul to survive it? The freezing cold blasted into him as he threw the carriage door open. The driver halted the horses as Renwick hastily jumped out into the muddy drifts of half-melted slush.

"Renwick," Thador barked, lurching from his seat as Aneryn rubbed her eyes. "Where are you going?"

"I need some fresh air," Renwick growled. Book still in hand, he stomped up the hillside. Even with his fae healing, the wound in his thigh screamed at him. When Thador began to follow him, he shouted, "Stay with Aneryn."

His guard paused, seemingly debating ignoring his orders, but he turned back. The cold eased his panic, the chill numbing his pain. Whorls of mist billowed behind him as he plodded onward up the mountain. A rising buzzing kept trying to erupt from beneath his skin, and he tried to hold it in like the urge to vomit.

"No, no, no," he groaned, swallowing back the blinding pain in his temple. His finger fumbled for the vial in his pocket.

Heart pounding from exertion, he reached the summit just as a vision exploded into his mind. The blank hillside warped before his eyes, morphing into a giant castle. Spires and bridges flickered into being as rambling roses blasted up from the frozen earth. All at once, a palace erected before him, covered in sweet-smelling flowers and beautifully carved stone. His fingers tingled as he looked up to the highest tower. A little face pressed against the windowpane, waving a chubby hand down at him. He knew her, this child. Somewhere in his heart, he knew her just as he knew the beautiful fae behind her, holding her up to see. Lifting his hand, he waved up at her just as the castle vanished.

He stood alone on the frozen mountainside once more, the smell of blood still clinging to his skin. His heart shredded into a million tiny pieces. He looked up through the gloom of clouds to where that little face had been. He knew then that he would do anything to protect them. Salvation be damned. He'd tear down the sky for the glimmer of hope that she would survive. Even if it would damn him to never be worthy of her love.

He clutched the book in his hand to his chest while his other shaking hand grasped for the vial in his pocket. He uncorked it with his teeth, eager to forget all that he had just seen. Bringing the potent liquid to his lips, he took a bitter swig and sealed his fate.

*I hope you enjoyed Renwick's story! If you enjoyed this novella, please consider leaving a review, telling a friend, or sharing on social media! -A.K. xx*

# PATREON

Join A. K. Mulford's Patreon to receive ARCs, book mail,
access to the Mountaineers discord server, spicy artwork,
and brand new novellas!

# ACKNOWLEDGMENTS

Thank you to all the amazing readers who wanted to hear more of Renwick's story! This novella was born out of many walks in the rain and listening to my "90s Feels" playlist.

Thank you to all of my amazing patrons! I love creating worlds with you! A special thank you to Krista Montes and Kait Hudnall. I can't wait to take you on more adventures in Okrith!

To my #Booktok fam, thank you for being the most incredible, kind, and uplifting community! And thank you to everyone in the High Mountaineers reader group. It is an absolute joy connecting with you!

To my amazing team of alpha and beta readers, thank you for helping make this book the best it could be!

Thank you to Sara from Sara Johnson editing and to Norma from Norma's Nook Proofreading!

Thank you to Holly Dunn for the design for the Map of Okrith and thank you to MiblArt for the cover design.

# ABOUT THE AUTHOR

A.K. Mulford is a bestselling fantasy author and former wildlife biologist who swapped rehabilitating monkeys for writing novels.

She/they are inspired to create diverse stories that transport readers to new realms, making them fall in love with fantasy for the first time, or, all over again.

She now lives in Australia with her husband and two young human primates, creating lovable fantasy characters and making ridiculous Tiktok videos.

**www.akmulford.com**

# ALSO BY AK MULFORD

### The Okrith Novellas

The Witch of Crimson Arrows

The Witch Apothecary

The Witchslayer

The Witching Trail

The Witch's Goodbye

### The Five Crowns Of Okrith Series

The High Mountain Court

The Witches' Blade

The Rogue Crown

The Evergreen Heir

The Amethyst Kingdom

### The Golden Court Series

A River of Golden Bones

A Sky of Emerald Stars

Made in United States
Troutdale, OR
10/17/2024

23847369R00061